He'd said he loved her, that they were twin flames, so how could he reject her now?

Marinda felt weak again and struggled to breathe. Ramian stood on a higher platform facing Gavin. The beautiful redhead sneered at Marinda.

The redhead turned her back to Gavin. He placed a triple strand of pink pearls around her neck and started to fasten them.

Marinda's vision went hazy and she gasped, grabbing Svelty's shoulders for support. "Hell, no."

Gavin lurched toward her but stopped, the flash of concern replaced by a blank mask.

"Gavin?" she screamed.

He didn't look at her. "I reject the land dweller," he said.

She felt ill and sank to her knees onto the hard marble. He was discarding her, just as Nate had.

Exhaustion dropped over her like a blanket. She welcomed it, and shut her eyes. She longed to sleep and curled her naked body into a ball on the hard marble floor.

Best dream ever...

Marinda Rhinehart loathes the cold and has been scared to swim ever since she fell through the ice of Lake Huron when she was a teenager. So why is she standing with Gavin, the most handsome man she has ever seen, in a frigid icy place in a formal wedding-type ceremony, and giving up her V-card for mind-blowing sex she's only read about in books?

Except it isn't a dream...

When she wakes up in her apartment in Gainesville, Florida and makes plans to go back to Michigan in the winter for her aunt's funeral, dream guy is at the airport. She doesn't believe he's real and still has major trust issues after she was dumped in college by her long-term boyfriend who was on another date at the time.

Gavin insists he's not a dream and that she has really joined with him. He doesn't tell her he must battle Ramian, a ranking leader at his home under the waves in the Granite Cliffs, to allow her to take her place with him in his homeland. And it must be her choice. Can she give up her life on land and trust her heart and life to a man she barely knows in an alien place? And can he keep her safe from Ramian's hatred?

KUDOS for *On Thin Ice*

In *On Thin Ice* by Tara Eldana, Marinda has moved from Michigan to Florida because she is always cold ever since she fell through ice into the lake when she was a teenager. Now she is having dreams about a man who lives under the sea. When her aunt dies, Marinda goes home to Michigan for the funeral and discovers that her dream lover is not a dream after all. But can she conquer her fears and go with him, or are they doomed to ever love from afar? With wonderful characters and lots of hot spicy love scenes, this is my kind of book. I heartily recommend it. ~ *Taylor Jones, The Review Team of Taylor Jones & Regan Murphy*

On Thin Ice by Tara Eldana is the third in her Mermaid series. Marinda Rhinehart has moved from the chilly Michigan winters to the sun of Florida, where she hopes she will no longer be cold. Then her aunt dies and Marinda goes home for the funeral. However, at the airport when she arrives in Michigan, she sees a man she has only seen in dreams. At least she thought they were dreams. Gavin, her dream lover, claims to be real and tells they are betrothed. He wants her to leave her family to come with him under sea and take on her fish form—which she does in some embarrassing places. *On Thin Ice* is a cute and clever romance with plenty of hot sex scenes. What's not to love? ~ *Regan Murphy, The Review Team of Taylor Jones & Regan Murphy*

ACKNOWLEDGMENTS

To the fabulous members of the Greater Detroit Romance Writers of America for paying it forward.

To the staff at Black Opal Books for making it happen.

To my husband and family for their support and encouragement.

On
Thin Ice

Tara Eldana

A Black Opal Books Publication

GENRE: STEAMY ROMANCE/PARANORMAL ROMANTIC SUS-
PENSE

This is a work of fiction. Names, places, characters and incidents are either
the product of the author's imagination or are used fictitiously, and any re-
semblance to any actual persons, living or dead, businesses, organizations,
events or locales is entirely coincidental. All trademarks, service marks,
registered trademarks, and registered service marks are the property of their
respective owners and are used herein for identification purposes only. The
publisher does not have any control over or assume any responsibility for
author or third-party websites or their contents.

DEDICATION

For my mother, who read to me.

Chapter 1

Marinda Rhinehart was always cold.

That was why she took a job down south in Gainesville, doing public relations for the University of Florida after she finished her master's in business from the University of Michigan, although she knew nobody in Florida.

She'd fallen through the thin ice on Lake Huron during a mild winter as a kid and, since then, never quite shook the cold that settled in her bones.

But here she stood, her breath forming plumes of smoke as she stood waiting. Her wavy blonde hair that she never wore down in the Florida humidity hung down to her shoulders. A necklace of dark blue stones encircled her neck.

A man wearing a purple robe appeared from behind a

cliff. He had long black hair secured back from his face, eyes the color of the Atlantic Ocean, and a clean, hard jawline. He smiled and came toward her, taking her hands in his warm ones.

"You are not cold, yes?" His voice was deep and melodic.

English, she thought, was not his first language.

"I'm not cold," she said, although it made no sense.

"Come with me, Marinda."

She nodded.

This had to be a dream. The man who held her hand had broad shoulders, a toned chest, and lean flanks. She felt she knew him.

He looked down the icy cavern to the narrow channel of water. "I am Gavin."

He led her past the cliffs, through a series of winding chambers that looked like granite, to a great hall filled with people wearing robes similar to Gavin's in shades of red and gold. Nobody else wore white or purple.

The crowd spoke a language she didn't recognize. He stopped at a raised platform in front of a woman with white hair and an unlined face. Her eyes were the same color blue as his.

He took hold of Miranda's hands, holding both of them, and smiled into her eyes as the woman spoke. He said a few words then stopped. She understood none of it.

Everyone watched her.

What was she supposed to do?

He squeezed her hands. The woman placed her hand on Marinda's shoulder. Her eyes were kind.

"Will you be with him?" she said.

Why not? This was only a dream.

"Yes, I will be with him." Whatever that meant.

He took her in his arms and kissed her, brushing his firm lips over hers, coaxing them open. She had been kissed before, but never like this. His tongue plunged in and out and she met him thrust for thrust.

The crowd cheered. He drew away from her, winked, and then lifted her into his arms. He strode through a series of granite hallways sprinkled with ice crystals to a chamber with a huge oval shaped purple crystals that threw white light.

Morsels of shrimp and other things she didn't recognize were arranged on oblong shells. He set her down, shrugged out of his robe, and stood clad in only a loincloth. He was lean but muscled, with a swimmer's body with washboard abs and a smooth chest. His black hair fell loose to his shoulders. She couldn't stop staring. What was wrong with her?

Looks weren't everything and could blind you to a guy's true character. She'd learned that in college. Nate, her boyfriend for two years, dumped her in Dooley's while he was on a date with another girl.

But this was only a dream, so it didn't matter, right?

He put his hands on his shoulders and unfastened the back of her gown. It slipped to the floor.

She was naked. She shivered, but not with cold. He pulled her against him, his erection pressing into her backside.

His breath felt warm against her ear. "I am not a dream."

His hands moved from her shoulders to cup her breasts that suddenly ached for his touch. His lips moved to her nape, and he bit gently as he tweaked her nipples into stiff pebbles. She moaned, and he chuckled.

He took her hand that she'd clenched into a fist, laced his long fingers through hers, and pressed it over his loincloth.

"Feel?" he said. "No dream."

He murmured a word she didn't understand. "Means cherished one. Darling," he said.

"Darling?"

It was all so real. She waited for his touch and the room to dissolve into a different nonsense dream where she was late for an exam for a class she hadn't attended all semester or her teeth to melt then wake up in her apartment in Gainesville.

"No dream, darling."

How did he seem to know what she was thinking?

"Sea dwellers must share thoughts without speaking under in the waves."

"You know what I'm thinking?"

He turned her to face him. "Yes. It is essential to survive. Will you be with me?"

Did he mean sex? She couldn't meet his blue-green eyes and stared at the cleft in his chin. "You look like a movie star," she said.

"Movie star? Is Brad Pitt?"

She laughed. "Where is this place?

He captured her chin so she looked into his eyes. "Iceland is closest human land mass."

Human?

He looked at her solemnly. "You will be with me."

Heat flooded her cheeks. "I've never—" She bit her lip. "I'm still a virgin."

He caressed her flaming cheek. "I know this, darling. You please me greatly."

He kissed her as he had in the great hall and her nerves dissolved. She returned his kiss and wound her arms around his neck then slid her fingers into his hair. He deepened the kiss and lifted her into his arms and onto the bed. He stood and took off his loincloth. She stared at his erection.

Based on what her girlfriends said, and her dismal attempt with Nate, Gavin seemed huge. Her nerves flared.

"Marinda?" He said her name melodically so it sounded like part of a song.

"Your voice, you could be a rock star."

His mouth quirked into a smile as he fed her a piece of shrimp.

"Rock star, like Men and Monsters?"

She nibbled the shrimp, that tasted better than anything she'd had in Florida, and giggled.

"Of Monsters and Men?"

He stretched out next to her and circled his long finger around her nipple, drawing closer and closer to the
tip. He flicked it, teasing it into a hard point. She arched
into his touch, and he replaced his fingers with his mouth,
laving her nipple with his tongue, then sucking hard.

Heat flooded her core, and he slipped his long, blunt
finger inside her slick channel. He found her G-spot as he
bit gently on her nipple and she came hard, screaming his
name.

He removed his finger and entered her in one quick
thrust. She felt a pinch of pain as he breached her barrier.

He stroked her cheek, his eyes filled with concern. "I
cause you pain."

She pressed a kiss into his palm. "Just for a moment
and not much," she said. "Best sex dream ever."

He looked sad for a moment and surged inside her,
stretching her. "No dream." His thumb caressed her bundle of nerves as he eased in and out of her.

He wasn't wearing a condom and she wasn't on birth
control.

"Gavin, stop." He did, with his fullness inside her. A
nerve twitched in his cheek.

"I'm not on birth control."

"You don't want my seed to make baby?" He sounded hurt.

Her heart ached. She caressed his shoulders. "No—yes, I want babies someday, when I'm married." And awake.

His expression softened. "We are joined, mostly."

She looked down to where he was buried inside her.

He smiled. "I mean you are my...you are bonded to me..." He said a word she didn't understand. "I wait for you to be my lady, um, wife."

He waited for her?

She had a dim memory of when she fell through the ice when she was seventeen and someone with a low melodic voice under the frigid water helped her and said he would wait for her.

"Yes, darling, I wanted to bring you with me then but the council said I must wait."

"What is this place?"

"Translates to English to Granite Edges, Cliffs. It is under the waves in what you call Arctic Circle."

Under water? She was under cold water?

She couldn't stand the cold and never got in cold water. She couldn't breathe.

He pulled out of her and held her tight. "Marinda, don't." He sounded panicked.

c⁄ɔc⁄ɔ

She jerked awake and sat up, drenched in sweat, alone in the apartment.

The dream had been so vivid and she felt stretched and different *down there.*

She could still feel her dream lover's touch, still smell his essence of fresh water, and taste his kiss.

She peeled off her sweaty T-shirt, grabbed a towel, stepped into the shower, and noticed a tinge of red when she pressed a washcloth into her tingling sex. She must be spotting, although she never had before between her cycles.

Sighing Gavin's name, she let the water wash over her skin.

ᐸᔆᐳ

Gavin paced before the Ruling Council. Ancient doctrine dictated that he would lead the Council as his sire Garon had done. The Council could challenge this if he was deemed incompetent or unstable. His sire perished in the depths after he helped a pod of whales stranded in waters far from the Granite Cliffs because the portal breaching time and space, which would have shortened his journey back, was damaged.

"He is obsessed with this land dweller who has fear of cold and water," Ramian said. The Council appointed Ramian to rule after Garon perished.

Gavin's mother, Laria, who held a seat on the Council, looked at him and made a sign for him to stand still.

"She is my lady," Gavin said. "I have seen it in the crystals."

"She must join with you of her own free will," Ramian sneered.

Gavin forced himself to keep calm. "I know this,' he said.

"You are not fully joined," Ramian said.

"You state the obvious," Laria said. "Do we not have other matters? Shall we let Gavin see to this? We can spare him for a time."

"The land dwellers are melting the ice in the polar caps," Ramian said. "Gavin is needed to ensure—"

Laria cut him off, which was permissible because she had co-ruled with her mate, but was deemed too stricken with grief to continue to do so after he perished. She had fought and won to keep her seat on the Council.

"There is nothing urgent. Go to her, my dearest son."

She extended her hand toward him and chanted ancient words of protection. The others on Council joined in, including Ramian, who glared while he did so.

Gavin grabbed his lucky knife, slid it into his sheath, and made his way to the portal.

⚬⚬⚬

Marinda scraped her hair into a ponytail to face the Florida humidity that seeped up the coast in early March. She was running late because her mom phoned early with the sad news that her Aunt Lola, her mother's twin sister, had lost her battle with ovarian cancer.

Lulu, Marinda's mother, said it was a relief to know her twin did not suffer but Marinda could feel her mother's deep grief and said she would come home to Michigan as soon as she could. She would finish up the details for the alumni fundraiser dinner and ask Brenda, her boss, for time off.

She hoped Brenda wouldn't give her any crap about it. Marinda wanted to take a couple weeks off unpaid, which would strain her budget, tight with student loans, but her mother needed her.

She sent Brenda an email as soon as she got to her desk that she wanted to see her, thinking it would be better to ask her face to face, as Brenda's emails were terse and bitchy.

Brenda's reply pinged. *Nine-thirty my office.*

Marinda had a half hour. She called the catering firm with the final head count for the fundraiser and followed it up with an email. Then she triple-checked a press release and sent it to Brenda for her approval.

Taking a deep breath, she walked to Brenda's office and explained her situation.

Brenda frowned. 'We don't give bereavement for aunts or uncles."

We? "I'd take it unpaid."

"You'd be gone for the alumni dinner."

Sweat trickled into the small of her back. "Everything should be all set. I talked to the catering firm just now and gave them the head count."

Brenda stared at her computer screen and waved her off dismissively. "Do what you have to do."

No sorry for your loss or even eye contact. Bitter bile rose in Marinda's throat. She swallowed it and choked out, "Thanks."

She hurried toward her office. Her friend Sara, who worked with the large donors, stopped her.

"Rin, what's wrong?"

Marinda's tears fell then. Sara pulled her into the break room and sat her down at a corner table, her eyebrows knit with concern.

"My aunt died," Marinda said. "The one who was fighting cancer. I asked for two weeks, unpaid, and Brenda was a bitch."

Sara rolled her eyes. "Big surprise. I asked for time for my sister's wedding in Hawaii and she acted like I was stealing from college endowment fund."

Marinda rubbed her tears away. "I know, right?"

Sara stood up. "Let's get you out of here. Anything you need?"

Gavin, she needed Gavin.

Marinda hugged Sara. "I think I'm good. Thanks for listening."

෬෬෬

"Gavin?"

His mother stopped him before he entered the portal. "Did you look in the crystal so you know where she is? She has left Florida."

"Where is she?"

His mother looked displeased. "You are impatient, my son. You must leave nothing to chance."

He ached for Marinda and, in his haste, he did not look in the crystals.

"Your sibling did," Laria said.

His female sibling Svetlana was so young when their sire perished she had no memory of Garon. She ran to Gavin and he swooped her into his arms.

"What did you see, Svelty?"

"She is sad, Gav. She is on a journey in the machine that goes above the waters and the land." She held her hand up. "She's going to a place like this with fresh water all around."

He set his sibling on her feet. "That is where she fell through the ice," he said.

They went to the hall of crystals and he saw where her journey would end.

"You must not be rash," Laria said. "You must do things with careful thought."

He put his hands on his mother's shoulders. "I will do so. She is mine. We are life mates. I have waited so long."

"Time is different on land," Laria said. "It will be different for her here."

He tamped down his impatience. "We will help her, won't we, Svelty?"

His sibling nodded. "Ramian gets red in his face when mother talks about it."

He chucked his sister under her chin. She giggled. "That's because he is filled with foul air and he must let it out."

"You must be back before the equinox," Laria said. "The portal will not function properly and Ramian's term of office is up shortly after that."

"He wants you to join with Zephoria," his sister said. "I heard it in my fin class. She doesn't live here either. I don't understand."

"Ramian thinks that would strengthen alliances among sea dwellers," Laria explained.

"I will have Marinda or I will have no one," he said.

"You have fourteen earth rotations, dearest son. She must come back of her own free will."

He kissed his mother, then his sister, on their foreheads. "You may alter time and space only once," Laria said.

Gavin nodded.

"I will miss you, Gav," his sister pouted.

He swooped his small sister into his arms. "I have been gone longer checking dolphins."

"I know. I always miss you," Svelty said.

He set her down next to Laria. She enfolded her daughter into her arms.

He raised his hands over their heads and chanted ancient words of love and protection. "I miss you, too, Svelty, and you Mother."

They extended their hands and repeated his words.

He winked at his sister. "Thank you, Svelty."

He checked that his knife was sheathed then stepped into the portal.

Chapter 2

Marinda rode the escalator down to baggage claim. Why had she brought so much luggage? She could have been picking up her rental car if she had just brought a carry-on. It was only a two-hour flight but she felt drained. She needed to focus on her mother.

She trudged toward the baggage carousel.

It was empty.

She stared absently into the crowd forming around the conveyor.

Her eyes fell on a man with broad shoulders and dark brown hair like Gavin.

She looked away. Gavin wasn't real.

Broad-shouldered guy scanned the crowd and his gaze fell on her.

Holy hell.

She forced the heated air in the terminal into her lungs. The guy was the living image of her dream lover.

He winked at her, the way dream Gavin did, then started walking toward her.

It must be her nerves. She was seeing someone who wasn't real. She staggered to a row of chairs and sank down, trying to keep her breathing steady.

"Marinda, you are unwell." The guy sat next to her. Great. Now she was hearing voices.

He put his hand on her cheek. She stared at him, struggling to form words, when the luggage started coming down the carousel.

Her two red suitcases tied with black and white polka dot ribbon slid past. "That's mine."

"Which?"

Even his voice was how she remembered from her dream.

"Red with black and white ribbon."

He sprinted to the conveyor. A man in a suit handed him one of her cases.

Gavin thanked him and the man in the suit nodded.

So someone else could see him?

He hoisted her cases without using the handles or wheels as though they weighed nothing.

He wore work boots, jeans, and a black T-shirt. He had tied his hair back. More than one woman checked him out.

He stood in front of her. His blue-green eyes looked sad. He squeezed her icy cold hands. "I am sorry that your mother's sibling perished." He let go of her hands and pulled a necklace out of his pants pocket that looked like sapphires. Lifting her hair aside, he fastened it around her neck then settled it over the collar of her blouse. "Jewels look like your eyes. They remind me of you after you leave me."

Leave him?

He tugged on the necklace, his eyes lit with gold. His gaze held hers. "Gems are symbol we are joined." He pulled her to her feet and into his arms, oblivious to the crowd. His mouth settled over hers, his tongue seeking entry. She opened her lips and he deepened the kiss. She hung boneless in his arms. He smelled and tasted the same as her dream lover.

She pulled away from him. "I have to go," she said.

"You must be with your mother in her grief. I know this. We go."

We?

She pulled the handles up on her suitcases and put on her slim winter coat. The wicked March wind she felt each time the outside doors opened had already begun to seep into her bones.

"I have to pick up the rental car," she said. He managed both her cases as they made their way to the counter and she filled out the paper work.

Her mind was swimming but she forced herself to

concentrate on the tasks at hand. He insisted she wait inside while he got the car. He didn't wear a coat and the chilly air didn't seem to faze him.

He pulled up and slid out of a Mustang. "You wish to drive, yes?" He put her cases in the trunk then got into the passenger seat.

She had planned to stay at a hotel close to her parent's three-bedroom condo because her sister Olivia and her husband and two kids were staying with her parents. Marinda and Livvy thought her five-year-old Sophie and two-year old Ryan would be a welcome distraction for their mother.

Gavin leaned forward, pulled a long sheath out of his work boot, pulled a knife out of it, and set it on his lap.

Holy hell.

"How did you get that through the metal detectors?" She pulled away from the rental car area and into a spot in short-term parking. She had to have some answers before she trusted herself to drive. She turned toward him. "I don't understand. Nothing makes sense."

He pulled her across the console and into his arms. "I know this," he said against her ear. He took hold of her chin so she stared into his bright green eyes. "I am impatient, always with you. I wait so long." He claimed her mouth in a quick kiss. "You wait for me too, I think. You were virgin." He tightened his arms around her. "I am different from land dwellers."

Land dwellers?

"I will show you this soon. We are twin flames. I see you are my lady in the hall of crystals." He tugged on her necklace. "We will join complete when we return to Granite Cliffs." He looked deep into her eyes. "If you wish. We must leave before equinox to make journey.

Equinox? Wasn't that in two weeks? She shook with nerves and cold and blasted the heat. Beads of sweat formed on Gavin's upper lip.

She pulled out of his arms and sat in the driver's seat, still too shook up to start driving.

"You wish to see your mother, yes?"

"I don't trust myself to drive."

❧❧❧

He felt her grief and fear in every cell of his being. He had to ease her pain. He had one, maybe two chances to alter earth time and space while he was on land. His beloved was longing for her grieving mother but his words muddled her head.

He was not sufficiently skilled to drive the machine without more practice.

He wrapped her fingers around the circle used to steer the machine. "Hold onto me, Marinda, and to this. You must think of where your mother is, the destination you would drive to, and send your thoughts to me."

She looked at him in disbelief then shut her eyes.

He could see a row of structures near water and chanted. She gripped his hand.

When they had settled, he told her to open her eyes.

She gasped. The machine sat in front of a one-story earth dwelling with water behind it.

Her eyes were wide. "How?"

He got out and went around to where she sat to open her door. "We talk later." He pulled her into his arms and kissed her. He sighed as she pressed against him.

"Marinda?" a female voice called out from the entrance of the structure.

"I have to go," she said.

He took hold of her waist. "We go together."

She started to shake and he chanted words close to her ear to calm her.

She leaned back against him. Did she know how suited she already was to live in the Granite Cliffs? Or how she was meant for him?

"Yeah, Liv," she said.

They walked to the female Gavin took to be Marinda's sibling and they embraced before they walked inside.

"This is Gavin," Marinda said.

He smiled and nodded at her sibling. "Sorry for your sadness."

"He's from Iceland," Marinda said.

"Holy hell, Rin. You could have said something."

⸙⸙⸙

Her sister stared at Gavin, slack-jawed, before she recovered. "I'm Olivia."

She led them inside and pointed at her husband. "That's Jack. Our children are Ryan and Sophie. The kids flanked her mother on the couch who was looking through a box of photos. Her father wrapped her in a hug and she wept softly.

"How is she?" she whispered in her dad's ear.

"Better than we thought," her dad murmured.

"Dad, this is Gavin."

Her dad thrust his hand toward Gavin. "Robert Rhinehart."

Panic shot through her. Did they shake hands where he came from?

Seeming to read her thoughts, Gavin winked at her and thrust out his hand. She sagged in relief then sank to the floor to hug her mother.

"I'm so sorry, Mom," she said.

"Scooch over, Soph, let Auntie Rin sit."

Her niece protested until Gavin crouched down so he was at her eye level.

"Show me where drink water is," he said.

Marinda stifled a gasp at his choice of words but Sophie chortled with laughter. "Drink water, you're silly."

"Show him, baby," Lola said.

Gavin kissed her mother's cheek. "Sorry," he said. He held out his hand to Sophie, who pulled him into the kitchen with Ryan toddling behind. "Watch your brother," Liv called.

Marinda sat next to her mom. "Marinda Renee." Her mother looked toward the kitchen. "Why didn't you tell me?"

The lie that sprung to her lips was partly true. "Aunt Lulu was sick, you had so much on your mind."

"Spill it, sister," Liv laughed. "I always wanted to say that."

"Tough girl." Jack laughed and put his hands on Liv's shoulders and looked at her with so much love, Marinda's chest hurt.

Did she dare hope for that with Gavin? Or had Nate stolen her ability to trust anyone with her heart? And how could she explain who he was? She didn't even know.

"He's from near Iceland. This happened fast," she said, which was mostly true.

"What does he do?" her dad said.

Crap.

Her dad, an attorney, could smell a lie a mile away.

Gavin, with Sophie on his shoulders and Ryan at his heels, stood behind her. "I study geology under the oceans," he said.

"A scientist," Liv said.

Her dad looked at Gavin steadily over his reading glasses "Where did you go to school?"

Gavin peeled Sophie off his shoulders and expertly lowered her to the ground. "Ice-U."

"University of Iceland?" Jack said.

"Lots of field work," Gavin said.

Things grew quiet. Livy got the kids ready for bed. Her mother looked exhausted.

"We're going to go," Marinda said.

"Call me," Livvy mouthed.

Marinda kissed her parents goodnight. Gavin took her hand and led her into the chilly March night.

When they got to the hotel, they passed by the pool to check into their room. There was a hot tub, and she longed for a soak to ease the cold from her bones.

"We go to the water?" Gavin asked.

"Yes," she said, fishing her bathing suit and cover-up out of her cases. Gavin put his knife and a long crystal into the small room safe and pocketed the key.

He had nothing else but the clothes on his back. She changed in the bathroom. He wore his T-shirt and jeans.

"Do you have something to swim in?" she said.

He winked and threaded his fingers through hers. She grabbed the room key and they walked to the pool.

"It closes at ten," the clerk at the front desk said as she stared at Gavin.

They had a half hour and the pool and hot tub to themselves. He kicked off his boots and shrugged out of his jeans. She pulled off her cover-up.

Holy cow. He was commando save for a loincloth.

His bare ass was fine. She darted a look at the front desk clerk, but she was gone.

"Gavin, somebody will see," she hissed.

He peeled off his shirt, revealing his broad shoulders and toned chest with that smattering of dark hair she remembered from her dream.

"No dream, darling."

How did he know her thoughts? He pulled her toward the pool when she longed for the hot tub.

"Come," he said, slipping into the pool. "You will understand."

She sat gingerly on the top step as he glided back and forth under the water, doing three laps without coming up for air. He swam up between her legs and fused his mouth to hers. The kiss went on forever. When he released her mouth, they were in the deep end.

She grabbed onto the side. "Gavin, I don't swim in deep water."

"I teach you." He kissed her again and moved their bodies under the water. She struggled briefly. He deepened the kiss and she was lost to everything but him. He took his mouth from hers and put his hands on her waist, propelling her pliant body back under the water to the shallow end.

She was breathing under water.

Holy hell.

He moved them back to the steps. She pushed her wet hair out of her face. How did that happen?

He kept hold of her waist and settled her between his thighs. She could feel his erection. He nuzzled her neck.

A tingling feeling started in her toes and travelled up her legs. He took hold of her chin so he could look into her eyes. "I—we—are different."

He undid the ties on her bikini bottoms, then her top. He kissed her again, and she met him thrust for thrust. When he released her, she felt different.

She stretched out and felt something flutter. She glanced down and screamed. Her legs and feet were gone.

She had a tail like gossamer in shades of crimson and deep blue that matched her necklace.

She fluttered her tail and squealed with joy. It felt so right.

"Is your destiny," he said against her ear. He tugged on her necklace. "You like sea form."

He let go of her then and submerged, taking his sea form, resplendent in shades of green and gold. He swam to her and pulled her into the deep water. They surfaced, keeping sea form. She rubbed her breasts against his chest and frowned.

How would they make love like this? He pinched her waist and she felt tingling in her tail, which disappeared, leaving her feet and legs. She stared at his strong thighs. His erection pressed against the apex between her thighs.

"Take sea form when I wish. And you may only do so when I allow it until we are fully joined." He nipped at her ear then nuzzled her neck. "You must learn your fins."

The hotel clerk tried to open the door to the pool, but she couldn't. She hollered through the glass. "It's ten. They have to close."

"Rules of humans," he laughed.

"Just a minute," Marinda said.

Where was her bathing suit?

Unconcerned with his almost nudity, Gavin hauled himself then her out of the water and picked up two towels. She wrapped one around her sarong-style. He wrapped his towel around his waist, picked up his clothes and boots then unlatched the door.

The clerk couldn't keep her eyes off him.

"Holy cow," she said softly as they walked past.

He took the room key out of Marinda's nerveless fingers, opened the door, and then dropped his clothes inside, and used his boots to keep the door open. He swooped her into his arms and carried her inside, pulling the door shut behind them.

"Is human thing, right?"

Her towel came loose as he eased her on the double bed, lay next to her, and stared at her naked body.

Suddenly nervous, she reached for the bedspread.

He took hold of her hands and held them over her head. "Why are you shy with me?" He said a word after that she didn't understand. What did it mean? He let go of her hands and traced her jawline with his finger before he moved his hand to cup first one breast, then the other. He repeated the foreign word again. "Means my heart."

Could he read her thoughts?

"Yes. Is necessary for sea forms in the depths."

Could she read his thoughts, too?

"Now, if I wish it. When we are fully joined, our thoughts will be as spoken words."

"That's a shame. I love your voice. And when you sing—"

Holy hell. She thought such terrible things about people sometimes, like her boss and about Nate. He dumped her so fast, like he was changing his shirt.

Gavin's hand stilled. His eyes narrowed. A muscle twitched in his cheek. "Who is Nate?"

She put her hand on his cheek. Was he jealous? "A guy, a jerk, in college. We were serious, or I thought we were until we weren't. He means nothing to me."

His erection teased her sex. "He did not touch you. You were virgin."

She arched against him. "He was with a different girl the same night he broke up with me. Livy thinks he was with her all along. I meant nothing to him."

He surged inside her, hitting her elusive G-spot. She moaned.

"He is fool. And I am glad. You are only mine." He pulled out and thrust again, skin to skin. He wasn't wearing a condom. She tensed.

"Gavin, I'm not on anything."

He looked puzzled.

"I'll get pregnant. We'll make a baby."

Looking sad, he caressed her cheek. "Is not possible on land. Only in Granite Cliffs for sea forms."

He surged again, hitting the back of her womb. She moaned.

He stared into her eyes. "You don't want babies?" He stayed deep inside her, filling her, watching her. His eyes blazed gold.

"Yes, I want babies."

And she realized she did. She clenched her muscles around him to prove her words. He groaned and pumped into her, hitting each sensitive nerve perfectly until she dissolved into nothing, screaming his name as he poured himself into her.

He collapsed on top of her then rolled them on their sides, spooning her. How could this happen so fast? It felt like she had known him forever.

She sank into exhausted sleep.

Chapter 3

Spring sunshine blazed through the window. Gavin's head was between her legs. He sucked hard on her pearl of nerves as his fingers found her G-spot. She came so hard, she blacked out. When she came back to herself, he was on his side next to her. She reached down to stroke him. He was hard.

"Hi," she said.

He smiled and pumped into her hands.

"I like hi," he said.

She giggled. "Hi is a greeting, like hello, good morning, bon jour."

He removed her hand and rolled her so she was astride him.

"How many languages do you know?" she said.

"Six. Not good. I was bad student. Thinking about

girl I save in icy water then leave above the waves."

"That was you?"

He lifted her and brought her down slowly, working himself in her slick, tight channel, inch by inch. He surged inside her, filling her. "Da, yes. I saw you in the crystals before that. Saw your danger."

She shut her eyes.

☙☙☙

He needed to look into her blue eyes and watch them turn stormy gray when she came. He needed that connection with her as much as he needed the essence of pure water. "Marinda?"

She opened her eyes, clear as arctic skies.

"Look at me, I want to see you."

She put her soft hands on his shoulders, and he sank deeper. He could look at her forever. He would look at her forever. Sea forms joined until they merged their essence into the sea at the end of their existence, after hundreds of earth revolutions.

Only when the cast of her eyes glazed gray and she dug her nails into his shoulders, marking him, did he allow himself to come, filling her with his seed. He reluctantly eased out of her. She burrowed her head into his chest and he pulled a blanket over her to keep her warm.

She had such a strong aversion to cold. How would she adjust to life in the Granite Cliffs under the ice of the

Arctic Circle, where the air and waters were cooler than other cities under the waves and certainly colder than Florida?

She grew up here, feeling the bite of winter winds from the deep lakes surrounding the land mass, but her plunge though the thin ice made her fearful of the cold and of water.

If only he had taken her back with him when he saved her instead of handing her back to her humans and Nate, who had hurt her.

Gavin could have told the elders it was the only way to save her. Then her fears wouldn't have taken such strong hold.

She would have grieved for her family, she would grieve for her family now when she left them—*if* she left them.

It had to be her choice. Would she, could she, love him enough to leave everyone and everything she knew? Could he let her go if she couldn't?

Her electronic device buzzed then pinged. She lifted her head from his chest then trailed kisses across it. "That was amazing." He grew hard again. She kissed the tip then lifted her beautiful face. "Is it, are you always?"

He laughed. "When you are near me, da, yes."

She took him in her mouth. He groaned. She pulled away at looked at him in alarm. "Did I hurt you, I've never done this."

"No darling, it is different." Damn his laziness in his

language classes. "The opposite. You please me beyond measure."

She smiled and took him in her mouth again. He thought his heart would burst with love. She looked up at him through her long brown lashes.

"You do not have to do this," he said.

"I want to. Tell me how."

His encounters with female sea forms faded to nothing. He hadn't wanted them. There was only Marinda since he saw her in the crystals, only her face he'd seen during those other hazy encounters. "Nothing you do will be wrong darling," he said.

She sucked on his tip then licked his length, cupping his balls. Was this what the ancients called heaven?

Ready to spill his seed, he pulled her away. He couldn't allow himself that privilege yet. He spread her legs apart and sucked hard on her sensitive bundle of nerves till she rained honey on his tongue. He held her in his arms, stroking her soft skin.

Her electronic device vibrated again. She reached for it. "I better check that." She pressed her thumbs to send messages. "Are you hungry? They have food at the buffet for another hour."

∽∾∽

What does he eat? She'd nibbled deli sandwiches at her parents' but she didn't see him eat anything. He stood naked, save for his loincloth. He held out his hand. "We eat."

"Clothes, we have to wear clothes."

He shrugged and pulled on his jeans, then boots, leaving his chest magnificently bare. She pulled sweatpants and a hoodie on, not bothering with underwear. Her necklace nestled under the sweatshirt between her breasts.

Liv had noticed it last night but Jack distracted her before she could ask about it. Marinda pulled her hair into a messy ponytail and stuck her feet into socks, then sandals.

Gavin, still gloriously bare chested, pocketed the room key, slipped his crystal then knife into his boot, and then reached for the doorknob.

"No," she said. She picked up his shirt and lifted it to her nose, inhaling his scent before she gave it to him. It smelled like water from the hose in summer time, crisp and cold air, and something else that was only him. "No shoes, no shirts, no service."

He pulled it over his head. His mouth quirked into a smile. "Human rules."

They walked to the buffet table. Outside strong winds swirled snow flurries. She shivered.

He looked at the scrambled eggs, sausage, bacon, oatmeal, apples, and pastry on the buffet line and frowned.

"Sit down," she said. "I'll get you something." What would he eat?

She took an apple and brought it to him. "Try this." She learned toward him and whispered although most of the business types seemed oblivious. "You bite into it." She bit it and handed it to him. She turned and filled a bowl of oatmeal and drizzled it with honey. She grabbed a pastry for herself and noticed the suit at the next table staring.

Gavin had eaten the entire apple, core and all.

"He lost a bet," she said, faking a laugh. "Try this," she whispered, pushing the bowl of oatmeal closer as the suit shook his head and stared at his cell phone.

She needed caffeine, a lot of it. She poured herself a mug and Gavin some orange juice and turned back to him. He held the bowl of oatmeal to his lips and slurped it, leaving the spoon untouched. The suit laughed and an older couple stared.

"He lost a bet," the suit said.

"Must have been some bet," the older guy said.

Marinda forced another laugh and nudged Gavin.

"Go back to the room," she said, handing him the key. "I'll bring some stuff back."

He smiled and eased his body out of the chair. Every female pair of eyes in the room followed him. Who could blame them? His ass looked fine in those jeans, but they were his only clothes he had. Her family would notice. Her hands shook as she sipped her coffee.

She was a shit liar. Her mother was distracted in her grief but her dad, Livvy, and Jack would ask questions. She could say the airline lost his luggage.

They needed to go shopping.

The March wind rattled the windows. She gulped her coffee then grabbed a plate before they closed the buffet.

Bacon, everybody liked bacon, right? She took a hard-boiled egg, a pancake and spread it with strawberry jam and a dollop of whipped cream. She grabbed two sets of silverware for Gavin's dining etiquette 101 class. She took it back and barely covered the basics of what and how to eat when her phone rang.

"Surprise." It was Livvy. "We're in the lobby. Sophie and Ryan want to try out the pool and Mom needed a break.

Crap. "Give us a few," she said.

Panic tightened her chest muscles and she couldn't breathe. Gavin took hold of her waist and sang her name over and over. He pulled her face into his neck and she inhaled his scent, which soothed her jagged nerves.

"You are calm?" he said against her ear.

"Livvy and the kids are here. They want to swim."

Her panic returned and she gasped for breath.

"They swim, darling, we stay dry."

An idea took shape. "You stay here. I'll say you think you're coming down with something and don't want to get the kids sick, and I'll say I have my period."

He looked puzzled.

"Monthly cycle?" she said. "What happens when females don't have a baby." Her hand strayed to her flat stomach. "The first couple days, most women stay out pools."

"Soon, Marinda, when we are fully joined, you will have my baby."

Her knees turned to water and she would have sunk to the floor if he didn't have such firm hold of her.

The phone buzzed with a text from Livvy.

ETA?

"I've got to go." She didn't want to move. She burrowed her face into his chest for a last fix before she pulled away and looked into his eyes. The tenderness she saw there unraveled the last shred of her reserve.

"I love you," she said.

He closed his eyes, as if he was in pain. "At last you give the words to me." His eyes blazed gold. "I also feel this love. I wait so long, Marinda."

Her phone pinged again.

He kissed her on her forehead. "Go. I am down with something, and you may not swim."

"Bye," she said.

"What is bye?"

"Until later. Speaking of bye, we have to have to 'buy' you different clothes. You look incredible. But you can't wear the same stuff every day."

He frowned.

"Is not our custom," she said.

"Your sibling waits and so will I."
She grabbed the key and left.

Chapter 4

The crystal in his boot vibrated. He pulled it out, unconcerned. He was off eco duty. He placed it in the middle of his forehead and froze in dread. It was Laria. She was sick with worry. His small sibling had gone missing and she was last seen near the portal.

"Is she with you, my son?"

"No, Mother."

In equal measures, his heart was breaking, and he was seized with fear. He had to go through the portal to search for Svelty. Sea forms inexperienced in bridging time and space could get trapped in the vortex. He had to leave Marinda.

He sighed. "I'm coming, Mother."

"With Marinda?"

"I don't know." He knew she couldn't leave her family until the ritual of grief for the spirit of their loved one had finished. He couldn't leave without explaining. He took the second key and went to the pools. He opened the door and called her name, forcing himself to smile at her sibling.

"He must be feeling better," her sister said as he came to where they sat.

"What is it, Gavin? You look upset," Miranda said.

He took hold of her, made excuses to Livvy, and rushed her to their room. "I must leave. My sibling, Svelty is gone. She may be caught in the portal. I will not ask you to go back with me."

Tears welled in her vivid blue eyes. "The funeral, my mother—when will you come back?"

He took hold of her chin. "You must journey to Granite Cliffs in ten earth rotations if you wish to be with me. Sea forms in Granite Cliffs may bridge time and space once, perhaps twice during each solstice and equinox. This will be two for me."

She grabbed his shoulders. "You're saying if I don't leave with you now, you're not sure you can come back for me."

He wiped her tears with his thumb. "We will find a way, my heart."

Her body shook with sobs. He backed her against the wall and lifted her, fitting her body to his. He claimed her mouth and pushed her pants down her legs. She stepped free of them then wrapped her legs around his hips.

He undid his pants and impaled her in one stroke. She was wet and ready for him, meeting him thrust for thrust. Her muscles clenched around him and he poured himself into her. He tugged her sapphire necklace free.

"Mine, Marinda. You are mine. Say it."

He couldn't leave her until the words left her lips. It was the second part of the joining ritual. The final part would happen in Granite Cliffs if she wished it to be so and could bridge time and space to get there.

"I'm yours."

He dropped his forehead to hers. "I must leave."

She wept. "I love you."

He eased her away from him. "I know, my heart." He took the crystal wand and pressed it to the bridge of her nose. "We must connect with this. You will see images. They are real. We are real, my darling. This—I—am your destiny. I see this in the crystal in the hall of records. But this must be your choice."

Her cheeks were flushed. He looked through the crystal to see if his sibling had been recovered but she remained missing. He held a sliver of hope that Marinda would come with him, but he knew her love for her family would not allow her to leave them in their grief.

He swallowed hard and walked away from her, feeling like a warrior must when an appendage had been ripped away. He had to keep Svelty's small face in his mind's eye so he could leave.

Still, he hoped she would follow. Her wrenching

sobs told him she would not. How could he keep moving away from her when his heart felt like it would burst apart? He clicked the door shut behind him.

❦❦❦

Marinda clutched the quartz crystal and shook with sobs. He was gone—again. He loved his family. She loved that he did. She went to the mirror and tugged on her necklace, looking for the clasp so she could take it off and put it in the safe, but she couldn't find it. Her face was a red, blotchy mess.

"Rin?" Livvy called from outside her door.

"Just a minute."

Gavin's seed dripped down her thighs. She moistened a washcloth and cleaned herself, reluctant to wipe his essence off her skin. She wet another washcloth, pressed it to her face and opened the door.

Her niece and nephew bounded in dripping wet. "I have to go to the bathroom," Livvy said, glancing around the room, looking puzzled. "I didn't want to drag them in with me." Sophie plopped her wet butt on the bedspread. "Where is Gavin?"

"He had to leave. His family needs him."

"I like him," Sophie said. "He's handsome."

Marinda put her arm around Sophie's wet shoulders. "I like him, too, sweetie."

Livvy popped her head out of the door. "Rin, I just started. Could you spare one?"

Shit. She was busted. She didn't have any.

"I just ran out," she said. "They sell some by the front desk. I'll be right back."

She looked around the hotel, hoping Gavin had changed his mind and stayed. Her indifferent heart and body had come to life, and he was gone as quickly as he came, like the March winds that ripped things apart with the promise of spring then simply died away.

The front door opened and she felt the cold in her bones, chilling her soul.

She paid the high price for a box of tampons and noted absently that her breasts felt fuller. She would have to put on a bra. Livvy had turned the TV on to a kid's channel. The kids sat entranced.

Livvy looked at her in concern when she handed her the tampons, then shut the bathroom door.

Marinda leaned back against the pillows on the bed and tried to take slow deep breaths to ease the tightness in her chest.

Livvy climbed into the bed next to her. "Where is he?"

She decided to stick with the truth as much as she could. "Family emergency. His little sister went missing. He had to go."

Livvy fingered her sapphire necklace. "This is amazing. From Gavin, right?"

Marinda nodded.

Livvy had worked for a jeweler when she was in college. "They're real, I think. And so large. Does it feel heavy?"

"No." It felt like it belonged there, like she was born to wear it.

"Can I see it better?" Livvy took hold of the necklace and eased it around her throat. "Rin, I don't see a catch." There was a thread of panic in her voice. She shuddered. "You can't take this off. If these are real, I can't even put a price on it. Someone could hurt you to get it."

"I'll keep it covered. Gavin said it was an heirloom."

The lie came easily but Livvy looked at her suspiciously. "You're a shit liar, Rin and Dad noticed it too."

"Shit liar," Ryan said.

"Don't say that, Ryan. Only grownups can say that."

Both kids got restless and asked to go back to the pool. Livvy gathered their stuff. "Come on, Rin. At least put your toes in the water. You've gone so pale."

Marinda picked up the room key. "All right."

Gavin said she couldn't take sea form unless he wished it.

Livvy stayed on the pool steps with Ryan. Marinda rolled up her sweatpants to her knees, sat her butt on a towel, and dangled her feet in the water.

Sophie splashed around just off the step wearing floaties on her arms.

"Mom wants us back for lunch. Then she wants us to

go with her to make the funeral arrangements. Jack will keep the kids."

"Watch me, Auntie Rin."

Marinda tried to smile. Sophie paddled up to her and took hold of her waist. Marinda felt her feet tingle and looked in horror as the tip of her beautiful tail unfurled.

Ryan squealed, "Auntie Rinny's a fish," before she could pull herself out of the water.

Livvy screamed.

Marinda frantically covered her tail with a towel.

The clerk from the front desk came toward them, frowning. "Keep it down or you have to leave."

Livvy hauled the kids out of the pool and shielded Marinda. "We're leaving, sorry."

"Aunt Rinny's a fishy," Ryan said.

Livvy laughed nervously. "Just pretend, buddy. Just a game."

Marinda felt her toes and peeked under the towel.

Her tail was gone.

They walked back to the room.

"What the fuck, Rin?" Livvy said.

ⅇↄⅇↄ

Gavin found Svelty wedged into a cache within the portal, shivering and weeping. He used the handle of his sheathed knife to create enough extra space in the cache so his sibling could wiggle free. She leapt joyfully into his arms. He eased them toward the channels of the Granite Cliffs. "Why did you do this, Svelty?"

"I looked in the crystals," she hiccupped. "I saw you with the young land forms." She squeezed her arms around his neck so tightly he had to tug them loose.

"So you wanted to play with them or did you think they would be more to me than you are?"

"Both." She muffled her answer against his shoulder. "Is Mother angry?"

"Our mother is scared. You must be in places she knows you are safe. And you and I are the only sea forms with the same mother and sire. Nobody else will take your place."

He navigated the final passages, his love for his sibling was the only thing that propelled him forward toward his home and farther away from Marinda, his heart and twin flame.

They stepped into the churning icy water and took their sea forms to move through the deep channels to the edge of the Granite Cliffs. Laria waited as they swam to the entrance of the city.

She took Svelty into her arms after they pulled themselves out of the sea. Laria beckoned him into her embrace before she pulled away. Her face was solemn.

She bent her head in in ancient thanks for their safe return. Svelty followed. He tried to chant the words but he could not. "This has cost you greatly, my dearest." Laria squeezed his hand and wept.

"You are sad because Marinda did not come and it's my fault," Svelty sobbed. She scampered away from them and ran through the caverns toward the great hall. He made a move to follow his sibling, but Laria stopped him.

"Svelty will be safe. There is a way, son, for your twin flame to come to you. It will be difficult for her. She must plunge through the ice into the water where you saved her. And it must be during the equinox. The sages say this is possible. You must make her understand this."

It would not happen. "She hates the cold," he said. "Is there something else?"

Laria squeezed his shoulder. "She is altered."

"What?"

She held a crystal to his forehead. He saw her tail unfurl in the pool. He stood as still as the cliffs that surrounded his home. His mother made soothing sounds as she did when he was still learning his fins.

"My son, she carries your seed. The sages are certain, although they did not think it was possible. They have since learned it has been reported that sea forms have joined with land dwellers in other cities in the alliance and have produced offspring. The males the land dwellers joined with rule their cities."

He gripped the hard edges of granite, panic coursing through him. "She is in danger on land, if her altered state is discovered."

"The sages believe the change began when you first

saved her, and breathed your life force into her soul."

They made their way slowly to the great hall.

"So when we joined here, when she believed I was a dream—"

"Yes," Laria said.

"But if she plunges through the ice, will both she and the baby survive?"

"It is not known, and she must be made to understand the peril."

He stopped. He would never see her or his child, unless he returned to land. And he would not be able to bridge time and space. He'd used up his allotments.

He would face peril in the seas if he went to her. There was no choice. He had to try.

"I must go back, Mother, through the seas. Immediately."

She took his arm to propel him toward the city. "You are rash. Sea forms can venture onto land but they require the essence of pure water. You know this. And you could not inhabit land indefinitely, although—"

"Although?"

"There is a report that a female sea form lives in the place the humans call Kauai, but this is not confirmed."

The humans had joined with sea forms who ruled their cities in the alliance. He had resisted taking a seat on the ruling council, although he could do so because his sire Garon had been ruler.

Gavin had grown bored with the endless machinations of the politics and Ramian's grandstanding.

His mother's thought came to him. '*You could change things and ease the way for Marinda.*'

He laughed. Sea forms could communicate without words. His mother did so with her offspring with great ease. He would need to guard his thoughts of Marinda around his mother.

She laughed softly.

❧❦❧

Marinda's mother was calm and composed as they sat with her uncle and cousin and made arrangements for her aunt's funeral. They went back to her parent's house, and she and Livvy sorted through photos while her father and Jack took the kids to the library. Their mother rested on the couch with her eyes closed.

"I had the most vivid dream," Lola said. "Lulu came to me. She looked beautiful and young, not sick. She talked about you, Marinda."

Marinda went to her mother and held her hand. "Me?"

"She said you would leave us to go to a place with cliffs, but not to be afraid, that you and your baby would be okay. She said you could visit us but your life would be there, away from us, and that it would bring you great joy. And we will miss you." Her mother wept. "It was so real. Are you pregnant?"

Marinda shook her head.

"Do you have plans to go to a place with cliffs? And where is Gavin?"

Livvy took her mother's other hand. "Gavin had a family emergency," she said.

"It sounded like he goes to remote places to do his work," her mother said.

Marinda took a deep breath. "Yes, and he wants me to be with him."

"Lulu said I had to be strong."

Ryan and Sophie burst through the door, followed by her father and Jack, who looked wiped out. Marinda felt the rush of cold air but for once, she didn't feel the cold. In fact, she longed for it. She felt ravenous and went into the kitchen in search of something, anything, to eat. There was leftover pizza and she ate it cold. Her stomach rolled and she ran to the bathroom and threw up.

Livvy opened the door.

"Stay back, Liv, I don't want you to catch whatever's got hold of me."

Livvy clicked the door shut. Her eyes flashed in anger. "You're a fish. And you are probably pregnant. I heard what Mom said. What the hell is going on?"

Marinda sat on the toilet seat. "You wouldn't believe me." Livvy wet a washcloth and pressed it to Marinda's cheeks. She felt like she was on fire. "Could you open a window?"

Livvy touched the sapphires nestled under her hoodie. "You detest the cold. Spill it sister. I'm a sci-fi geek."

Marinda cracked the window open. The fierce March wind gusted. "He lives under the sea." Her story spilled out and Livvy didn't speak until Miranda was finished.

"But I don't know if I can bridge time and space to go back." Her voice cracked with emotion. "How can I leave?"

Livvy hugged her. "Why can't he be here? He could do his merman thing in Lake Huron or Michigan. We're surrounded by water."

"I don't think it works that way." Marinda felt nauseated again.

"Crackers," Livvy said. "Try to keep something in your stomach."

"Girls?" It was their dad.

"We're coming," Livvy said, opening the door.

Her dad looked at her face and frowned. "You're pale. Is the window open?"

"I'm going to go back to my hotel," Marinda said. "I don't want to spread whatever this is."

"Sweetheart, you know you can always come to us for anything."

Marinda nodded, too choked up to speak. She loved these people so much.

Livvy steered her to the kitchen. "Crackers," she said.

Marinda ate the stack Livvy set in front of her and sipped weak tea. Feeling slightly better, she said goodbye and drove back to her hotel, stopping on impulse to buy a pregnancy test, although Gavin had insisted it wasn't possible until they were fully joined.

How was any of it possible?

She flipped on the TV. A scientist was talking about the polar icecaps melting and how it would have dire consequences to marine life, sea levels, and global temperatures, although no one could say for certain what those would be.

A sick sense of dread settled in the pit of her stomach. What would that mean for Gavin and those who lived in the Granite Cliffs?

She took out the pregnancy test, read the direction twice, followed them and waited.

Holy hell.

It was positive.

She carried Gavin's baby.

Would he ever know? Would she ever see him again?

She felt sticky and sweaty and wanted to soak in the tub. She usually didn't spend any longer in the shower than she had to and didn't take baths, ever, not since she fell through the ice.

She filled the tub and stretched out. Her nausea instantly vanished. Squeezing her eyes shut, she pinched her waist in the same spot Emma did. The tingling started in her toes and spread up to her waist. She opened one eye and squealed in joy. Her gossamer tail, resplendent in the shades of blue that matched her sapphires, fluttered in the water. This felt so right.

She loved her sea form and she loved Gavin, but she would never see him again.

She wept until she had no tears left.

Chapter 5

She weeps because she takes sea form and carries your seed," Ramian said. His eyes glittered with hatred. He hated land dwellers. His son had been killed in the sea by a torpedo during what the humans called World War II.

"She believes she will not be with Gavin again," his mother said. "That is what makes her weep."

"I do not accept that," Ramian said. "She must be here of her free will."

"I know this," Gavin said, clenching his fist. He wanted to slam his knuckles into Ramian's face.

"Send the images," Laria said. "I will ask again if anyone in the city will give you their leave to slip through the dimensions."

Gavin knew it was unlikely. Those who had no wish

to leave the Granite Cliffs had already bequeathed their passes to the adventurous sea forms. There were also passes in sacred reserve for emergencies for those who embarked on eco missions. The seas that sustained them for millennia also held great peril and many, such as Gavin's sire Garon, who had been ruler, had perished in the depths on such missions.

Unless they came to harm in the depths, sea forms had a life span of about a thousand earth years, although their childhoods spanned the same number of years as land dwellers, and gestation was faster. Upon reaching their full growth, the aging process slowed. Sea forms joined for life. Some males had taken more than one mate at one time, but this was not done in the Granite Cliffs. It was more common in ancient times among the ruling class.

In recent millennia, distinctions between the ruling class and populace had blurred, and those who wished to serve on the ruling council could do so by securing a vote at large.

Their governing system was described by some as a mix of the British House of Lords and House of Commons.

Gavin would do it and take on the mantle of leadership if he could ease Marinda's transition into her life with him in the Granite Cliffs, or if it would help to bring her here to him. Many of Ramian's dictates were antiquated. Gavin could change things. He had ideas how to stop climate change above the waves. Marinda would help to build understanding of land dwellers. He burned with new purpose.

"I'd like to take my birthright to a seat on the council," he said.

Laria looked relieved. "At last. You were meant for this, my son."

His heart and body ached for Marinda. To see her in the crystals, then to save her from peril when she fell through the ice, then wait for her and have her so briefly—if he didn't focus on something until the earth's equinox, when she could return to him, he would lose his mind.

"You must make her see what she must do if she wishes to be with you," Laria said. "Go to the hall of records and do this now. I will make the announcement to the council."

He embraced his mother then made his way to the hall of records.

ℰ✺ℰ✺

Marinda lay on her bed and stared at Gavin's crystal wand. She picked it up and put it on her forehead, near the bridge of her nose.

Vivid images came so fast, she felt dizzy. She saw the spot she had fallen through the ice. She saw herself breaking through the ice, on purpose, and plunging through the frigid water into Gavin's arms. Shadowy, dark images of them as they made their way through the deep frightened her. She saw them stop at uninhabited islands presumably in the Arctic, frozen, icy places where the seals frolicked.

They moved stealthily through the depths until they came to the Granite Cliffs. Gavin formed small bits of crystals into the number twenty.

Did he mean the date, March twentieth?

He'd mentioned the equinox before. That was three days away. Aunt Lulu's funeral was tomorrow. How would she make an excuse to go the family cabin on Lake Huron? Her parents had closed it up for the winter.

And how could she leave her family?

Gainesville had only been a short plane ride or two-day car ride away. Would she ever see her loved ones again? Would the new life inside her survive the journey if she chose to make it? Would her baby be in danger if she chose to live on land? Would she?

Gavin's blue-green eyes were filled with love and sadness. The images stopped, and she was overcome with exhaustion. She slipped into a dreamless sleep.

~∞~

The wind blew icy cold on the day of the funeral and she was sweating under her coat. They stood around her aunt's casket in the unheated room at the cemetery.

If she left, she would be dead to her family.

Her mother wept in her husband's arms.

How could she cause them more sorrow?

Her eyes filled with tears. She blinked them away. This was about Aunt Lulu, not her.

When the priest was finished, Marinda hugged her cousin Christy and Uncle John, then rode with Livvy and Jack to the wake.

Her mother was dry-eyed and composed. She had spoken to her twin every single day of their lives and she didn't leave her side after they'd called hospice.

Marinda was famished and devoured two plates of chicken, pasta, beef, and mashed potatoes. The banquet room was drafty, and she welcomed the chill.

If she stayed, she couldn't live in Gainesville. The thought of the wall of humidity she'd face this summer made her feel ill. She'd be alone there and pregnant, doing a job for a boss who treated her like garbage.

If she stayed in Michigan, she'd have to find a job and tell her parents she was pregnant, soon. Her hand strayed to her belly. Ending the pregnancy was not an option for her. It was all she had left of Gavin. If, by some miracle, she got the nerve to break through the ice and make the journey with Gavin to his homeland, she would be leaving her loving family to live in a place where she didn't know the language or customs and where she'd likely be viewed with mistrust at best and hate at worst.

Millions of immigrants had left their homes and faced that.

Her father sat next to her. "You look so thoughtful, Rinny."

She squeezed his hand. "I was thinking I could take a ride to the cottage tomorrow."

He looked shocked. "In this cold? Who are you and what have you done with my daughter?" He put his arm around her and squeezed her shoulders. "I'll give you the keys when we get back. I'm taking your mom to Aunt Lulu's tomorrow. John and Christy want her to take what she wants from Lu's things. Livvy can go with you."

Her sister was chasing after Ryan and Sophie.

Her father's chuckle sounded almost evil. "Jack can keep them."

"Dad, I thought you liked him."

Her dad shrugged. "He's okay. Paybacks are tough. You give your baby to some guy, yanno?" He studied her in full lawyer mode. "Which I guess will happen with this Gavin dude. What does an ocean geologist do, exactly?"

Ryan hurled himself at his grandfather, saving her from answering. "Hey, buddy," she said.

"Rinny's a fish," Ryan chirped over and over.

Livvy rushed over. "It was a game," she said. "We played in the pool at the hotel."

Robert ruffled Ryan's hair. "Marinda wants to go to the cottage tomorrow," he said. "Make it…what do you call it?…a girl's day. Jack can ride herd on the rug rats."

Livvy gasped and started to cough. Her dad handed Ryan off to her and thumped Livvy on her back.

"Auntie Rinny's a fish," Ryan chanted.

"Shhhh," Marinda said, but it was no use.

Liv stopped coughing and started to cry. Her father hugged her. "I know, baby, it's been a rough couple days."

ΦΦΦ

Marinda turned in her rental and Livvy drove her SUV to the cottage. They didn't speak during the hour-long drive but played the classic rock station and listened to the music their parents enjoyed, Bob Seger and Alice Cooper, both from the Detroit area, and some of their favorite Motown songs from Marvin Gaye and the Supremes on Livvy's CD.

Breaking the silence, Livvy asked if there was music in Gavin's home.

They pulled up to the cabin and got out of the SUV.

"He has a singing voice like a rock star, so I'm thinking, yes," Marinda said. "And they chant."

"If you do this, what do I tell Mom and Dad? And what about your stuff?" Livvy was shrieking. "Here's an idea, don't do it."

The wind gusted and Livvy turned her back against it. Marinda handed her an envelope. "Here's all my computer passwords and what I want you to do." She had barely any money in her bank account so that wasn't an issue. Marinda already sent Sara a text, asking her to ship her stuff to Livvy and Jack. And she mailed her resignation letter to Brenda and to the Human Relations Department at the college, citing pressing family issues.

Her student loans were in her name. Her parents hadn't co-signed, so they couldn't come after them for the money she owed. She huddled with Livvy, although she welcomed the bite of the wind skimming over the mostly frozen lake, even longed for it. "Tell Mom and Dad Gavin came for me." Which would be the truth, she hoped. "And whisked me away to Iceland so I could meet his family because his mother is ill. Then say I'm with Gavin working. I'll find some way to stay in touch."

Liv shivered and Marinda hugged her, infusing her with her new-found warmth. "I can't stay, Liv. What happens when my baby and I sprout tails in the water? We'll be in danger."

"You'll have to learn their language and customs," Liv said. "Some of them will hate you just because you're human."

"Gavin will help me," she said. But would that be enough? She felt suddenly cold.

"No point in going into the cabin, yet. It's cold as death in there." Livvy gasped after she realized what she said and set the thick manila envelope Marinda had given her in the back seat. The fierce wind tossed the fluffy white clouds across the vivid blue sky, the color of

Gavin's eyes. Marinda had to think of Gavin if she had any chance of doing this.

"They'll be pissed you didn't say goodbye. Dad will go into full lawyer mode and have him investigated when you drop off the face of the earth."

"Tell him Gavin does classified government stuff."

"You have answers for everything," Livvy screamed. "I could lock you in this car like I locked you in the closet so you wouldn't run away when you were six." She was in full-blown hysterics now. "I call bullshit. I'm not going to watch you go through that ice. Let him live here. You don't have to do this. It's insane. My sister is not a fish."

Marinda grabbed Liv and held her. "Shhhhh. It's going to be okay." She said it over and over, but would it? What if she plunged into the icy water, and he wasn't there? She was risking her own death and the death of her baby. What if the images she saw when she put the crystal on her forehead were nonsense dreams and nothing else? What if she was losing her mind? "Let's see what it looks like on the ice, okay?"

Livvy wouldn't budge so Marinda walked past the fencing that her parents and others along the shore put up each year to keep the sand from blowing away during the fierce fall gales and strong spring gusts. Snow still covered the beach.

Stepping gingerly to the water's edge, she slipped and fell on her butt.

"Don't you dare do this without hugging me good-bye and getting something in your stomach," Livvy said.

Marinda ran back to her sister and put her arm around her shoulders. Livvy stared out at the ice then pulled a thermos out of the long pocket of her coat. "Drink this, all of it. You don't know when…" Her voice trailed off.

Marinda pulled away and took a long swig. It was hot chocolate, her favorite. "I know this part sucks, Liv." She chugged down the rest, although it tasted chalky, then hugged Livvy.

Her mouth felt dry and she felt sleepy.

Livvy stood stiff.

Marinda grabbed hold of her. "What was in this?"

"Five milligrams of valium. My neighbor took it before she knew she was pregnant. It won't hurt the baby."

Marinda's arms and legs felt like jelly. She couldn't go into the water. "Why?"

Livvy hooked her arm around her waist and turned back toward the cabin. "Desperate times. He's not here. If he was here waiting for you, it would be different."

Doubts swirled like the blowing snow. Was he just like Nate, discarding her as if she was nothing to him? Did he decide she wasn't worth the trouble?

She let Liv lead her into the cabin. Her parents turned the heat down low during the winter. Livvy cranked the heat up while Marinda sank into a couch covered with a dusty sheet.

She embraced the damp chill while Livvy's teeth chattered.

Marinda shut her eyes.

Chapter 6

S he's decided not to join with you," Ramian said. His minions bobbed their heads in agreement. "Zephoria is willing to join with you. This would strengthen our ties to the cities in the alliance."

"She was tricked," Svelty said. "I saw it in the crystals."

Laria crouched down so she was eye level with her young female offspring. "What else, Svetlana?"

"Her sister with the young humans Gavin played with crushed a blue pill in a metal tube, and Marinda drank the liquid inside. She said she gave her the drink because Gavin was not there, and she is afraid that Marinda will perish in the waters."

Laria stood up and placed her hands on Gavin's

shoulders "You have one more rotation to safely bring her back, son."

Gavin wanted to crush his fist into Ramian's face. He wanted no part of Zephoria. He'd wanted to leave the Granite Cliffs immediately after he announced his intention to sit on the council but Ramian said he was needed for a quorum on a council vote because other members were checking on the thinning Arctic ice cap where the polar bears and seals lived. The vote had been on a routine matter that could have been postponed.

Gavin had to leave before the effects of the equinox waned.

Ramian held a pass through the dimensions—one that he would never use since he was excluded from eco missions because he was an elder and because he held no desire to venture above the waves. He hated land dwellers and blamed them for changing the climate on earth.

Ramian's mate Xenobia had perished on an eco-mission not long after she had given birth to their only offspring, a male. She had ventured to the Arctic ice cap to help the polar bears as they tried to make their way from the retreating ice to land and their food source, the seals.

The starving and delirious bears had turned on her and ended her life.

Gavin felt a spark of sympathy for the hate-filled elder. He, himself, would easily become deranged if Marinda was harmed. He clenched his fists behind his back.

"Your pass through the portal, Chairman Ramian? Would you?"

The elder waved his hand in dismissal. "No."

Gavin stared into the elder's lifeless eyes. "I love her as you loved your mate."

Ramian turned away. Svelty tugged on his robe. Gavin hoisted her up so she perched on his shoulder. She giggled then spoke softly in his ear. "Old Lonio will give you his pass. I heard his female offspring's young male say so in fin class."

His mother heard Svelty's words. "I think I know where to find him," she said. "Hurry, my son."

c/ɔc/ɔ

Marinda opened her eyes. She was drenched in sweat but her head felt clear and her limbs felt strong. Dry heated air blew through the vents.

Liv was wrapped in a blanket, asleep on the couch, oblivious to the texts from Jack that pinged on her cell phone.

Marinda had to move fast before Liv woke up.

She loved her sister but she loved Gavin, too. He gave her life when she slipped through the ice. She came alive with his touch. No other male, Nate included, stirred her like Gavin in every cell of her being. She longed to hear his voice, feel his touch, and for her own sea form.

She would find a way to come back to see her family. Closing the door softly, she made her way to the icy lake.

The thin ice cracked under her boots. She toed them off. Her jeans and shirt followed. She feel cold as the wind blasted over the lake. She touched her sapphire necklace. It seemed to strengthen her resolve.

Livvy screamed. "Stop."

Marinda's bare foot cracked through the ice and plunged into the frigid water. She couldn't stop her scream of shock. This had seemed better in theory that it actually felt. She wasn't as altered and attuned to the cold as she thought.

Could she do this?

Livvy gingerly picked her way across the ice, drawing closer and closer.

"Stay back. Love you," Marinda yelled.

She jumped, trying to widen the crack in the ice, landing hard on her butt. The crack widened. Fighting panic, she dragged enough air into her lungs as she could then dropped into the frigid black water. The water was deeper than she thought. She couldn't touch the bottom. She pinched her waist, but she didn't take sea form. She swam away from the shore until her lungs felt like they would explode. She sent Gavin her thoughts of love as she sank lower and lower, landing on something hard. A shipwreck? Then there was nothing.

ᏋᏯᏋᏰ

Gavin reached her seconds before her death, just as she landed on top of one of the ships on the bottom of the lake. He breathed his life force into her, and she came back to him.

She sent her thoughts to him. '*Is the baby okay?*'

'*Yes, my darling.*' He tugged on her necklace and freed her of her bra and panties moments before she took her sea form.

She grasped his arms. '*We must show Livvy.*'

He had depleted his reserves reviving her because she had been so close to perishing and time was precious, but he could not refuse her. They swam quickly back toward the crack she had made in the ice. He lifted her head above the water. She called her sister's name and her sister screamed, as if in great pain.

Marinda stuck her tail through the crack.

'*Come, my darling, we must go.*'

She turned to him, and he claimed her mouth, not because she needed his life force but because he needed her essence more than he needed the essence of pure water. He released her mouth reluctantly, took firm hold of her waist, swam for the deep reservoir that connected Lake Huron to the Hudson Bay, and slipped through the natural portal.

Marinda was weak. He unsheathed his knife and cut through some shallow ice close to a speck of land near the Baffin Islands. He remembered this place from an eco-mission and saw no signs of humans. He lifted Marinda onto the tundra and she drew long, deep breaths.

He pulled her onto his lap and settled her so her soft cheek rested against his neck as their sea forms faded. Her bare breasts felt warm to his touch. She sighed.

He chuckled. "You will not always need this like now when we are fully joined." He cupped her sex and she pressed herself urgently against him, shivering.

Little bumps indicating she was cold raised on her arms. "I won't?"

He lifted her into his arms sand carried her to a place of shelter he remembered from his last stop. She needed to rest. "You will take air into your lungs when we come to land but you won't need it like now."

She expelled a long breath and her face suffused with heat. "I thought you meant us." She flicked her tongue on his shoulder and bit his neck gently. "The way I want you."

They reached the structure. He set her down to force the door open then pulled her inside and into his arms. He kissed her. She caressed his erection. He groaned into her mouth, and then released her.

"You are mine." Her blue eyes looked like storm tossed seas. "And I will only want you. We will join until we cease to be."

She nodded. "Yes."

"You must say words, 'Forever, it is so.'"

She caressed his cheek. "Forever it is so."

He pressed his mouth into her palm.

She lowered her eyes. "Gavin, on land males and females, they profess love and fidelity but they go with others."

He cursed his laziness during his language classes. What did she mean? Why did she look so troubled? He moved them to a small bed in the corner of the room, eased her onto his lap, and took hold of her chin so he could look at her. "I do not understand. What is fidelity?" He thought it was about levels of sound.

"They pledge to be with only one person, then they let another person touch them. We call it cheating."

He sighed. "It happens in Granite Cliffs when sea forms join with those who are not their twin flame.

He tweaked her nipples. "If I joined with Zephoria as Ramian wishes, this could happen. But you and I are twin flames, darling. Twin flames join until they cease to be."

Her eyes went soft and she smiled.

He rolled so she was on top of him so her skin didn't touch the rough, scratchy fabric that covered the bed. "You are mine, Marinda. And I am yours as well."

ପ⁄ାଡ⁄ା

His erection nudged her sensitive bundle of nerves. She rubbed it against him and he said her name, sang it really.

Twin flames. He said sea forms joined for life un-less—

Zephoria?

She went still. The air chilled her skin. He said if he joined with Zephoria, he would not be faithful. If he grew tired of Marinda, would he cast her aside as easily as Nate had done?

She moved away from him.

He took hold of her waist. "She is nothing."

She flinched. He slid into her in one smooth stroke.

She'd forgotten he could read her thoughts. "Nobody is nothing," she whispered.

He pulled out and plunged into her slick channel, hitting every nerve perfectly. She moaned.

"My language skills, you say, suck. You must teach me. You will teach all of us. Zephoria, I do not love. She lives in the Golden City. Joining with her would strengthen ties for politics."

He lifted her and impaled her, hitting the back of her womb. The world fell away. There was only him. Would it always be like this? She spasmed around him, screaming his name before she went boneless. He emptied himself inside her and pressed his thumb on her sex. Unbelievably, she came again.

"Who is Nate?" he demanded. "You think of him when we join?"

She lifted her head from his smooth, hard chest and looked into his troubled eyes. "I was nothing to him. He ended things between us, and I saw him with another girl the same night."

"Girl? He touched a young female?"

She caressed the hard planes of his face. "No. We say girl to mean young woman. It's confusing."

He put his hand over hers, pressing it firmer against his cheek. "He is fool. You did not let him touch you. You were mine, even then." His eyes raked over her possessively.

"Arrogant, much?" she said.

He smirked, which made him more handsome, damn him.

"Who is this Zephoria? Is she beautiful? Does she want you?" *What breathing female wouldn't want him?*

He looked puzzled. "Want for what?"

She rubbed her nipples against his chest. "This, joining."

His lips quirked into a smile. "You think other female sea forms want me as you do."

She trailed her hand down his toned arm to his lean waist then grabbed his magnificent ass. "Yes, darling husband, I do."

"I am almost husband. We join once more in great hall in Granite Cliffs." She moved his hand to his cock. He caught her wrist. "Say it again, my darling wife. I love those words on your lips. I feel joined with you since you fall through the ice and before that when I look in crystals."

He let go of her wrist.

She trailed kisses down his taut belly. "My darling husband."

A thought wiggled through her haze. He knew how to play her body like an instrument. Had there been others for him? She had no claim on him before now, she had no right to be jealous.

But she was.

He lifted her and brought her down so he filled her completely. He thrusted, hitting the back of her womb. She gasped in pleasure and shut her eyes.

He tugged on her necklace. "Darling, you must look at me." He swiveled his hips and she saw stars, squeezing his shoulders hard, scoring his skin with her nails, marking him. "Yes, others after I see you in the crystals," he said. "At first, I did not accept it. I think it is what you call bullshit." He lifted her, sliding out of her before he pulled her down onto him. "But I only see your face and say your name. So I stop."

"I didn't know," she said, drawing herself up so he filled her even more. "I was half alive after I fell through the ice. I figured it was an after-effect. I didn't know you changed me. You made me yours, then, right?"

Feeling bold, she took control, rising up and down on his cock. He pressed his thumb on her sex and she swiveled her hips. He said something she didn't understand.

"English," she demanded, stroking his scrotum.

"Yes," he moaned. "Like that."

She rode him hard and they exploded together. She

tried to ease off of him but he held her tight. "Is rough, this part on the bottom," he said.

"Sit up," she said. The bed was covered in burlap and his back was rubbed raw. She stood up, feeling his seed run down her leg. She pulled the scratchy material back. There was a woolen blanket underneath. "Get up, darling."

He laughed. "You are bossy."

She cast the burlap aside. "Lie down on your stomach." He looked puzzled. She trailed her fingers over his toned abs and stroked his impressive erection. "Are all sea forms this large and always hard?"

He swatted her bottom. "No, and you will have to take my words. You will not see other males this way in Granite Cliffs."

He rolled onto his stomach. The skin near his shoulder blades was rubbed raw. She searched through the ramshackle cabin, thinking the fishermen that likely used it may have left some type of ointment. She opened some creaky metal cabinets and found a tub of Vaseline and spread it over his shoulders as lightly as she could. "Does it hurt?"

"No." His breathing became even and deep. He'd fallen asleep.

Her stomach rumbled and she looked through the cabinets again and found a tin of sardines. She could never stomach the thought of them before but she was ravenous.

She peeled back the metal lid and ate the oily bits with her fingers. She moaned. They were the best thing she'd ever tasted.

She sucked the oil off her fingers and forced herself to stop eating and leave the rest for him. He had to be hungry, too. She looked back through the cabinets, but there was nothing else.

What would she eat in the Granite Cliffs? She turned back to him.

He was awake. He raised himself up on one elbow.

She brought him the tin of sardines. "Here. They're wonderful."

"You are wonderful," he said.

She held one to his lips and he nipped her fingers before he swallowed it whole and sucked the oil off her skin.

She moved her jaw up and down. "You don't chew?"

He laughed low in his throat. "Not for things small. Like humans with oysters."

He took the tin from her, pulled her onto his lap, and held a sardine to her lips.

"The rest are for you. I scarfed half of them already.'

"Scarfed?"

"Ate."

"I will find food in the water. I take it without holding it in heat. You are not ready for this, I think."

What would she eat?

"This for now." He could read her thoughts. She kept

forgetting that. What if she was angry at him? All guys acted like assholes sometimes, didn't they? From what Liv said, she got pissed at Jack several times a day.

"You will not get pissed at me for being an asshole," he said.

He understood that?

He fed her the rest of the can, held his fingers to her lips, and stared into eyes. She licked his fingers clean.

Heat flooded her core. She wanted him so much. How long could they stay in this place? Wasn't there some sort of deadline before the equinox? What if someone saw them? They were naked.

He was hard and his erection nudged her backside. "I want to be inside you but we must leave if you are rested."

They'd barely slept but she felt energized and alive. She slipped off his lap and pushed him down on the bed, trailing kisses across his lean stomach before she took his rigid cock in her mouth.

He groaned.

She sucked hard and took him as deep as she could. He pulled her up and under him and plunged into her slick, tight channel. He pumped his hips fast and she came hard. He followed her and collapsed on top of her. His weight felt good and she didn't want to move.

He eased out of her and pulled her against him. "We rest short bit.'

"Why don't I feel cold?" she said.

He put his mouth on her neck and sucked hard. "Because you are mine."

He's marking me, she thought. "I love you," she said before sleep overtook her.

Chapter 7

He smoothed her dark hair back from her beautiful, delicate face. Would her love for him sustain her when she longed for her loved ones? Would she grow to love the Granite Cliffs?

Ramian opposed their union. He had but one vote on the ruling council, but how difficult would the old windbag make things for them?

She'd given up her whole life and everything she knew to be with him. Could he have done the same for her, if it were possible?

Some said a female sea form lived with a human male in the group of islands the humans called Hawaii. If that was true, she must be able to get the essence of pure water she needed from the depths from the sea that surrounded the small masses of land.

Would they be able to do the same in Michigan, which was surrounded by large lakes that connected to the sea? If so, they could visit her loved ones, although because she was altered to sea form, she would not age as the humans would. Time was different in the depths. In time, this would be obvious, raise suspicion and put other sea forms at risk. Maybe they could visit for a time.

He had so much to tell her. But they had to leave. It was easiest to slip through the ancient channel during the equinox when the earth was tilted just so. They had to leave.

He said her name in the melodic way that seemed to soothe her and caressed her soft cheek, rousing her from her brief nap. She sat up quickly, looking troubled.

"Gavin?"

He pulled her into his arms. Was she frightened? Did she not wish to continue their journey? His heart thumped hard as if he had swam without stopping for one complete rotation of the earth. She shut her eyes and rested her head on his shoulder, taking deep breaths. Was she inhaling his essence? Did he find it as intoxicating as he found her scent, vanilla bean laced with a cinnamon stick?

"I want to be with you," she said.

"You read my thoughts," he said. She had altered to sea form even further. Sea forms needed to read each other's thoughts in order to communicate in the depths.

"I thought I dreamed you, all of this, again." There was a catch to her voice, as if she was trying not to weep.

"Like before, when we joined in the Granite Cliffs the first time."

She'd given him her virginity with such passionate abandon. His cock, which was semi-hard whenever he was near her, was hard as granite to the point of pain.

But she needed something else from him just then. He sang her name and she went soft in his arms. He grew even harder.

"No dream, darling. The first time, in Granite Cliffs, you grew afraid. That is why you could not stay. You must be with me of your own free will. The ancients decreed it."

She moved out of his arms. Her eyes darkened to the color of the sapphires she wore around her neck, proclaiming to all sea forms that she belonged to him. "I think I remember I said, 'Forever, it is done.'"

He smiled and held out his hand. She grasped it and he led her out of the shelter to the water's edge. A strong wind blew and he drew her against him to shield her soft skin.

"I'm not cold, darling," she said.

He kissed her, savoring her taste and infusing her with his life force. He drew away reluctantly and moved them so her feet were near the break in the ice. He pinched her waist and she took her sea form instantly, sliding into the water with a happy squeal. He dove in after her and took firm hold of her waist. They had a long journey.

e/se/s

She opened her eyes and tried to sit up, but hands held her still.

Gavin, where was Gavin? She screamed his name, and he came into her line of sight. He put a hand on her cheek.

"Marinda." He sang her name the way she loved. "We are home," he said.

He smiled, but his eyes looked troubled.

Panic seized her. She struggled to breathe. Sea forms in long, flowing robes pressed crystals to her forehead, heart and pelvis. "What's wrong? Who are these..." She couldn't say people. She gestured toward the half-dozen sea forms that surrounded her. "The baby?"

"The baby is strong," he said.

"What is happening?"

"The portal, there was trouble," he said.

"It was Ramian, I know it," a childish voice said.

"Svelty," an older female hissed.

"These are healers," Gavin said. "We had to make a longer journey than I'd hoped. You had difficulty."

She tried to sit up, but she felt dizzy and weak. Her stomach rumbled.

He wrapped one arm around her shoulders and held a bite of shrimp to her lips. "You must take food."

Was it cooked?

He smiled. "Was specially prepared."

It tasted fresh and wonderful. He also fed her bites of something green she thought could be seaweed.

She giggled. She would never touch sushi at home. The room they were in was filled with clear crystals, granite and marble. This was her home now.

The sea form she knew as Ramian swept into the chamber. A male healer said something to him that Marinda couldn't understand. Ramian retorted sharply.

The female Marinda thought was Gavin's mother interceded, blocking Ramian from Marinda's sight. Marinda couldn't understand their words but she heard Ramian say Zephoria before he glared at her with hatred.

Gavin erupted and left her side to shout at Ramian.

"Free will," Ramian said.

A small sea form, a miniature female version of Gavin who must be his sister, tugged on her hand. "He is saying you are weak and should return to land where you belong. He says if Gavin joins with Zephoria, it will make the alliance stronger. What is alliance?" She didn't wait for an answer. "I do not like Zephoria," she said, crinkling her nose in distaste.

"You speak English very well," Marinda said, squeezing her hand.

The young sea form smiled sweetly at Marinda, revealing a missing front tooth. "I watch You Tube in crystals. I am good in language." Her smile faded. "Ramian says your loved ones are sad because you are here. He says you must know this because of free will, and Gavin says you must first be stronger." Her beautiful little face crumpled. "Gavin will be cranky like before you came back. I not supposed to tell."

"It's okay, I won't," she said.

Gavin's mother came to them and smiled shyly. "I am Laria. I give birth to Gavin and Svetlana. We call her Svelty."

Laria's hair was black as Gavin's but her eyes were lighter blue, nearly turquoise.

Gavin turned away from Ramian and came to her side. 'You are good?"

"Yes." She smiled. "I am getting to know your mother and sister."

He looked puzzled.

"His English sucks," Svelty said.

Marinda laughed and that seemed to please the healers. She pointed to Laria. "Mother." She pointed to Svelty. "Sister. Like Livvy and Lola."

His face darkened. He brushed his lips on her forehead. "I leave you short bit."

"Okay," she said.

He looked puzzled again.

Chapter 8

The sound of her easy laughter eased the tightness in his chest. He wanted to hear that sound to the end of his existence. He followed the narrow passages to the hall of crystals and looked into the amethyst then the quartz and saw the same scenes in each crystal.

Marinda's mother was in a bed with tube in her wrist. She wept and told a woman in a white coat her daughter had left her. In another scene, Livvy sobbed in Jack's arms.

Ramian sidled next to him. "She must know of this before she speaks final words to join with you."

Her soft heart would break when she saw this. He had thought he would be able to take her back to see her loved ones but she'd nearly perished making this journey.

How could he ask her to cause such grief to her loved ones and choose to be with him?

In time, her guilt would erode her spirit. If she wished to leave, she could slip through the dimensions and awaken on land as she had before.

But she would carry his seed.

She was altered from their joining.

Would she grieve for him?

She would be near her loved ones. Would her love for him fade in time? Would she grow to hate him?

He looked through the crystals, hoping to see the future. He saw her laugh with her loved ones the way she laughed with Svelty, the sound he longed to hear forever, with her in his arms.

But it would not be so.

He loved her too much.

He would reject her, cause her pain and humiliation so she would wish to leave.

Zephoria. She was in Granite Cliffs.

He forced himself to turn away from his heart, his twin flame, and make his way to Zephoria.

છ⁄૭છ⁄૭

Marinda stood up. Her head was clear and her arms and legs felt strong.

Where was Gavin?

Svelty tugged on her hand. "Come with me," she said.

Marinda looked down at her naked body. The other sea forms were clad in long flowing robes. "You can't cover yourself until you say final joining words," Svelty said.

Swell.

"I know a way no one will see," she said.

Marinda followed her through a series of narrow winding corridors etched into the granite. She had so much to ask Gavin about. They came to room filled with crystals of every color. Svelty looked into what looked like a huge amethyst and started to weep. "Ramian show Gavin wrong thing."

Svelty's little body wracked with sobs. Marinda crouched down and took her in her arms. "Shhhh. It can't be so bad, sweetie."

"It is. Gavin think you will be too sad away from loved ones and they are sad without you."

Marinda smoothed her hair back from her tear-stained face "Show me what he saw."

There was a clip of Livvy crying in Jack's arms. Marinda had been there when that happened. So was her mother. Livvy was going bat-shit crazy that she couldn't get the kind hot house roses she wanted for her wedding.

In another snippet, her mother was in the hospital after she had her hysterectomy. Marinda had just moved to Gainesville and her mother was in a lot of pain and weepy, telling her father she missed her.

"Your loved ones think you are with Gavin on work mission," Svelty said. "They not sad like this." Svelty squeezed her hand. "Stay in Granite Cliffs with us, Marinda. Gavin not cranky anymore."

"Take me where he is," Marinda said.

She followed Svelty through narrow corridors into a great hall, the room where she and Gavin spoke words of joining.

He stood on a platform wearing a purple robe next to a drop dead gorgeous female with auburn hair swept up of her face in an elaborate style who wore the same type of robe.

"What is happening?" she said.

"It has started," Svelty said. Her lower lip trembled.

Marinda felt weak again and struggled to breathe. Ramian stood on a higher platform facing Gavin. The beautiful redhead sneered at Marinda.

The redhead turned her back to Gavin. He placed a triple strand of pink pearls around her neck and started to fasten them.

Marinda's vision went hazy and she gasped, grabbing Svelty's shoulders for support. "Hell, no."

Gavin lurched toward her but stopped, the flash of concern replaced by a blank mask.

"Gavin?" she screamed.

He didn't look at her. "I reject the land dweller," he said.

She felt ill and sank to her knees onto the hard marble. He was discarding her, just as Nate had.

Exhaustion dropped over her like a blanket. She welcomed it, and shut her eyes. She longed to sleep and curled her naked body into a ball on the hard marble floor.

I love you, Marinda. Go back to your loved ones. Gavin's thoughts invaded her slumber. She forgot sea forms could do that, read each other's thoughts if they wished to.

Gavin loved her? But he rejected her publicly. Wasn't that akin to divorce? But they were not fully joined, only sort of engaged. Her eyelids felt like they had lead weights on them, and she shut them. Those images he saw made him think her family was distraught.

But had he always wanted Zephoria? Was this an easy way for him to have her?

She wasn't letting him off so easily. Her eyelids felt glued shut and her arms and arms and legs felt like noodles, but she struggled to stand and rubbed her eyes open.

She moved on shaky legs to where he stood and looked up at him. "You lie, Gavin. You look me in the eyes and tell me you reject me. I was perfectly fine till you invaded my life."

A lie. She should have drowned when she fell through the ice. She'd only been half alive since then, anyway.

"No," he screamed, dropping the strands of pearls.

He bowed briefly to Zephoria, murmured words in their language, then jumped down from the platform to where she stood.

He yanked off the robe he wore and dropped it over her head, tugging her sapphire necklace over the silk-like fabric. He took hold of her waist. "You not perish under ice. I should bring you here then, like I want, and make you mine."

He stood before hundreds of sea forms, wearing only a loin cloth, and glared at Ramian. Gavin swung her into his arms and carried her to the platform, where he set her on her feet while keeping firm hold of her. He only let her go when his mother handed him a purple robe.

"Never form that thought again," he said. He kissed her till she forgot everything but his taste, his essence of fresh pine and pure water, and his erection pressing into her. He drew his mouth away and took her face in his hands. The look of fierce possession in his eyes made her forget everything except him.

But she had something to tell him, didn't she? "I love you," she said.

The crowd murmured approval.

She gripped his rock hard arms. "The scenes you saw in the crystals, they happened a while back, not now. My family thinks I came with you on a work mission. They are not sad. Svelty saw."

"Svelty?" Gavin roared.

"She is right here," Laria said, gently nudging her daughter toward them.

"You are still cranky at me," Svelty pouted.

Gavin gently pulled on his sister's hair. "No, I am not. But you must say truth. I want what's best for Marinda."

Svelty bowed her head and chanted words Marinda couldn't understand. Gavin threw back his head and shouted joyfully then released Marinda to throw Svelty into the air as she chortled with laughter.

He set her down then lifted Marinda into his arms and spun her in circles, chanting words in the language of the sea dwellers.

"She must speak words," Ramian muttered, glaring hatred at her.

Gavin eased her down. He had said Ramian had lost his mate while she helped sea creatures disrupted by humans, and he blamed humans for the climate change now melting the polar ice caps and destroying aquatic ecosystems.

Humans were responsible.

Drawing upon her marketing skills, which she would put to good use for once, she faced the crowd.

"Many humans, land dwellers, do not like the melting ice and try to stop it in many ways. Many land dwellers plant more trees when they get cut down, reuse things already made, and make those who put bad things in the air and water stop. I will try to help land dwellers do this if you let me stay." She glanced at Svelty. "We'll find ways to put ideas on You Tube. I would be honored to call Granite Cliffs my home."

She knelt on the platform, facing Gavin. She took hold of his hands. Gasps and murmurs of approval buzzed through the crowd. "I am honored to take sea form. I ask to join with you, my darling, if you wish it. Forever, it is done."

Gavin pulled her to her feet and into his arms, claiming her mouth in a kiss that was almost punishing in its fierceness.

She reveled in the crush of his arms and his taste as he plundered her mouth. She'd given him words in front of all these beings so they all understood she chose to be here with Gavin. He said they were twin flames. What did that mean? And were they fully joined?

He lifted his mouth and smiled. "Yes, darling, fully joined. You are mine for always. His eyes looked almost silver.

She drew back from him, frowning. *But what about Zephoria?*

He sighed. "There is much I explain." He took hold of her chin. "Twin flame—that I must show you."

He'd read her thoughts. She kept forgetting they could do that. He swept her into his arms to a roar of applause and strode out of the great hall.

❧❦❧

Would this be their chamber? How much time had passed since they had come here? She felt Gavin's steady breath near her ear and guessed he still slept. His arm held her snugly around her waist and she was pressed firmly against his chest.

Her stomach rumbled. She never felt so hungry. He had taken her to heights, repeatedly, she'd never dreamed existed outside of the pages of the bodice ripper novels her Aunt Lulu used to love.

He chuckled then kissed her neck. Heat flooded her core and she was hungry only for him. Sighing, she went boneless in his embrace.

He nipped her ear. "We must feed our offspring. He grows cranky."

He?

Gavin rose from the bed and lifted a crystal placed near the chamber entrance. He picked up the purple robe he'd all but ripped off her when he set her down in the chamber and tossed it to her.

He stood magnificently naked and stepped into a loincloth before he opened the door. Two young males carrying platters piled with food set them on a log table and a young female brought a crystal decanter of peach colored liquid and poured them it into a single large goblet. He set the food close by the bed and settled her between his thighs. There were no eating utensils.

He held a bit of chilled shrimp flavored with a tangy sauce to her lips. She chewed it up and sucked the sauce off his fingers. He fed her a crunchy vegetable she couldn't put a name to and round, red juicy berries, followed by the succulent shrimp until she felt full and waved him off. He held his fingers to her lips and she sucked them clean. Heat shot to her core.

Would he always feed her this way? Would she always want him as much as she needed air to breathe?

"In the great hall, nyet, I will allow you to feed yourself."

Allow?

She moved away from him but he pulled her back against him, laughing. "Punk'd."

She groaned. "You watch too much You Tube."

"And yes to second thing." His thing pressed into her backside, held her hair aside, and sucked hard on her neck.

He's marking me, she thought.

Laughter rumbled in his chest. "Yes, I find I like everyone to see how you want me and how much I want you."

She swiveled in his arms. He turned his back to her. Her nails, she'd left scratches on his back and shoulders.

She traced one red line near his shoulder blade lightly with her fingers. "I'm sorry. Does it hurt? I'll be careful, I promise."

"No, and I forbid it," he said.

Forbid?

He looked at her sternly. "You must not hold back.

We are twin flames. Our desire is sacred. We will want each other until we cease to be."

He caressed her cheek and traced her lips with his thumb. "You not age like loved ones on land. We visit for a while..." His voice trailed off.

"Livvy knows," she said. "Not that part." A thought occurred to her as he divested her of the robe. "That's why you didn't get dressed when the food came, so they would see your back."

His lips quirked into a smile.

Would their child look like him? "You said 'he.' Do the healers know the baby is male?"

He shrugged. "They not say. But males born first most times."

He bent his head and suckled her breast. She nearly came. She threaded her fingers through his hair that hung past his nape and moaned his name. He moved his mouth to its twin and pinched the nipple still ached for his touch. She came screaming his name.

She shut her eyes in shame. He took hold of her chin. "Look at me, Marinda," he said it melodically, soothing her nerves. "What is it, my darling?"

"My screams, others must have heard."

He slipped a long, blunt finger in her slick channel. "Do not feel shame. Our wanting for each other, this is sacred. I wait so long for you." His erection teased her sex.

She had one more thing to ask him. "Our child, how

will he age?" How long would he be an infant? How would she mark time? There was no day or night here.

"Young sea forms age like land dwellers do until they finish last fin class." At her puzzled expression, he kissed her forehead. "Like when you fall through ice."

"So when we visit my parents, the baby will look nor—like he would on land, but we won't."

He teased her bundle of nerves and she quivered. "We could paint gray in our hair." He nuzzled her neck.

"Land dwellers do the opposite," she giggled. "They dye their gray hair."

He found her G-spot. She screamed her release.

Chapter 9

When her breathing returned to normal, he stroked her hair. "I do not like you to alter this."

He thrust inside her. She was slick and tight. Would he ever have enough of her? She worried her bottom lip. Her thoughts drifted to him. She was thinking he wouldn't want her when her belly swelled with the child and she had fear of giving birth in the Granite Cliffs.

He pulled out of her and sucked on her bottom lip where she had pressed her teeth. His hand drifted over her slightly rounded stomach. "I will want you always, especially when you swell with my offspring."

Her eyes grew wide. They reminded him of sea water sparkling above a cloudless sky. He could look at her—would look at her—forever.

"And the birth?"

He entered her slowly, rubbing his cock against her nerve endings. She gripped his shoulders. "Our healers are more advanced than those on land," he said. "No disease here."

She went rigid. "Disease?" She sounded panicked. "What if I brought you disease? She wiggled beneath him. "Let me up. I should be quarantined." She sobbed. "Svelty. What if I made her ill?"

He plunged deeper inside her, hitting the back of her womb, and kissed her, moving his tongue the same way he was moving deep inside her. He pressed his thumb to her pearl of nerves and felt her spasm around him he emptied himself inside her.

When she calmed, he said her name in the melodic way he knew she loved and explained that the healers had ensured she carried no diseases from land when she arrived in the Granite City. He tried to make light of the peril she'd faced when he had trouble moving through the closest portal and they had to swim through the depths to reach Granite Cliffs. He had to revive her with his life force repeatedly because she was a new sea form not used to the rigors of long sea travel. He didn't tell her that had she perished, he would have relinquished his life force to the depths as well to follow her spirit. He didn't wish to draw breath or the essence of pure water without her, even knowing the pain Laria and Svelty would suffer in their grief.

He looked into her beautiful, trusting face. "You were reborn, darling, under my touch with my life force as wholly sea form. Means you can only stay on land for short times."

"You're saying I was gone, that my human life perished in the depths."

He nodded and chanted the ancient refrain of thanks. "This means you are mine. You affirmed your free will in the great hall."

Her eyes flashed stormy gray. "If I perished, how could I have returned to land when you rejected me for Zephoria?"

He stiffened. "You would have awakened on land as you did before. But you never take sea form, even if I come for you."

"So we could never be together?" she said.

"Da, yes."

She struggled against him. "You stupid male."

Anger as he had never known coursed through his being. "Stupid?" Still inside her, he hardened. Her beautiful blue eyes widened. He captured her small hands that had been pummeling his chest and held them over her head. He pumped inside her, finding the rhythm that pleasured her the most. "Stupid with love for you," he grated. "I believed Ramian's treachery."

He hit her G-spot and she came hard.

"I knew your tender heart could not let your loved ones suffer."

He emptied his seed inside her as she went soft in his arms. He released her delicate wrists and she took told of his face. "I'm stupid with love for you, too," she said. "But we must talk about things and make decisions together. I insist."

He tugged on her necklace. "Insist?"

She licked her lips. "It means—"

He kissed her lips, swollen from his kisses. "I know insist." He chuckled. "You will insist much, I think."

She delighted him beyond measure. He chanted ancient words of thanks.

She looked perplexed. "Gavin, your words, all of this, you must teach me."

He took hold of her and rolled so she was astride him. "I will, my darling, I will."

And he did.

c/ɔc/ɔ

Marinda held their squirming son as the holy ones chanted for his naming ceremony. Candles flickered in the great hall, reflecting in the quartz, amethyst, aquamarine and topaz crystals, giving the space an ethereal quality.

Grayson was an active six-month-old. She had insisted Gavin devise a way for her to mark earth time in the depths and her brilliant mate had done so.

Otherwise, she would float through her existence in

her new home in a mist of love for her mate, child, Laria, and Svelty and lust for Gavin.

She could do no wrong where he was concerned and she'd had to insist he tell her when she goofed up and did something not in keeping with the customs of the Granite Cliffs. She still had trouble believing her life here was real and feared she'd wake up in her tiny apartment in Gainesville.

Gavin stood next to her, resplendent a purple robe, the same shade as the one she wore. He took hold of her and put his mouth to her ear, taking care not to disturb her elaborate undo complete with jewels that Grayson kept making a grab for. Gavin chanted ancient words of love, as he always did when he knew when she was feeling out of her element.

"I will show how real this is, my darling, when we finish."

Laria and Svelty wanted to take Grayson to the little sea form pool and care for him when the ceremony was over. Svelty had even devised a way for them to Skype with her family through the crystals when the waves were right.

Talking with her parents proved tricky. She told them that she and Gavin had eloped, and Gavin's job meant they traveled aboard ships all over the world. Gavin promised they could safely travel through the portal to visit them in Michigan closer to the winter solstice, in two months, before the ice thickened on the Great

Lakes. She missed her family and her family missed her.

Gavin said it would be okay. That they would find words to soothe them.

He lifted Grayson out of her arms and high above him to the infant's delight. "Do not be afraid, darling," he said. "It will work out. We will make it so."

Laria beamed up at Grayson. "Your sire does that just as his sire Garon did," she cooed to her grandson. Gavin settled Grayson in Laria's arms. Grayson used his chubby fingers to make his sign for Svelty. He caught sight of his bubbly auntie and chortled with joy. Laria murmured words of love in the language of the sea dwellers.

Gavin lifted her in his arms and made way to their chamber as applause erupted. Would she ever get used to Gavin's PDAs?

He chuckled and sealed their chamber shut.

He always kept her guessing. Would he take her quickly to her release or make love to her for hours so she begged shamelessly for her release? Would he be masterful or allow her to explore his body however she wished?

They could not read each other's thoughts in this regard, only general intent.

She smiled. He never disappointed her. His power over her made her feel weak, but he had shown her that she held the same power over him. She chanted the ancient words of love she'd asked Laria to teach her to surprise Gavin. He was pleased. His smile curled her toes.

She would seek ways to make him smile like that for the rest of her existence.

"Portia says you are progressing in fin class," he said.

She wrinkled her nose at him. "I like it best when you teach me."

Gavin would show her the hidden caverns among the cliffs he and his fin mates had swum to in order to hide from the elders and avoid chores. She and Gavin would pull themselves from the sea, take land form and make love. At these times, he was masterful and she reveled in his possession. She ached for it now.

He sighed. "My duties." He slipped off their robes, pulled her against him and kissed her nape. He flicked his thumb against her erect nipples. "And your duties," he said.

Putting her marketing skills to actual use, she produced video clips that aired on You Tube to persuade humans to stop climate change. She also cared for Grayson with help from a sea form version of a part-time nanny.

Gavin moved his hand lower to cup her sex and slid his finger into her slick channel. She clenched her muscles around his finger and he groaned.

As a member of the ruling council, he was not required to take eco missions that took him away from the Granite Cliffs for more than one earth rotation.

She giggled. She was thinking as a sea form.

"Da," he said, following her thoughts. He pressed his thumb to her pearl of nerves and she came, screaming his name.

He said words in his language then switched to English. "You are mine. Forever, it is done."

She turned to face him, moving so his had stayed inside her. "You are mine," she said as she pulled his erection free from his loincloth. "Forever."

�૭ઈ૭

Gavin stood apprehensive near the water's edge where he first touched Marinda under the water as she slipped her clothes off. Her sister held Grayson, naked under the blanket she'd insisted on covering him with, although they'd insisted that Grayson, like them, did not feel the cold.

The low winter sun broke free from the clouds and Marinda turned her face toward the thin sunlight.

Could she leave land and her family to journey back to the Granite Cliffs with him? Contrary to what they first believed, the healers said she and Grayson would adapt to living on land, if they chose to stay.

But he could not.

He could only come for short periods of time.

He watched, feeling helpless, unable to ease her pain, as Marinda wept when she embraced her parents before they'd left them. Marinda told them Livvy would drive them to the airport, where they would fly to Iceland and board a ship.

Her father had asked persistent, probing questions. It had been difficult to satisfy his queries.

Now, with Livvy, Marinda stood naked. Gavin took Grayson out of Livvy's arms and turned his son's face toward the dwindling sunlight.

"You going to hug me or what?" Marinda said.

Livvy sobbed and Marinda wept.

Livvy took her sister in her arms. "You don't have to l—leave," she whispered, not realizing sea forms could hear sound at greater frequencies than land forms.

Could she leave such love? Marinda made no move to break free from her sister, though he had told her it was crucial they reached the portal in one earth hour to ensure safe passage to the Granite Cliffs.

How could he rip his twin flame away from her loved ones?

She sent her thought to him—*Free will, darling.* She kissed her sister on her cheek and entwined her small finger with her sister's small finger.

"Pinky promise," Marinda smiled. "We'll be back."

The tightness in his chest eased. She lowered her head and chanted ancient words of love for him and an invocation for safe travel.

"Bring her back, Gavin," Livvy said.

Marinda turned fully to him. He kissed her, infusing her with his life force, then drew them into the water.

Livvy watched them take sea form. "Holy hell," she squealed.

Gavin held Grayson with one arm and Marinda with the other.

"Forever, it is done." Marinda smiled. "Take us home, darling."

And he did.

THE END

About the Author

Tara Eldana is an award-winning staff writer for a weekly community newspaper chain in metro Detroit. She became hooked on romance fiction when her eleventh grade English teacher rejected the book report she wrote, saying the book was much too easy for her, and insisting she read and report on Daphne du Maurier's *Rebecca*. Eldana had read Margaret Mitchell's *Gone with the Wind* that previous summer.

Eldana took a long road through J-school, graduating from Oakland University in Rochester, Michigan in '95.

She loves the romance genre and loves letting her characters take control of their stories. Eldana is a member of the Greater Detroit Romance Writers of America.

Check out her other titles, *Under the Riptides*, *In the Depths*, *Double Dare*, and *Reclaiming Lexi* at taraeldana.com and visit her on Facebook.